Love Songs
A MUSICAL

by Steven Cagan

SAMUEL FRENCH INC.   60%

Presents
Logo 100%
LOVE SONGS
A Musical

by Steven Cagan (75%)

(PLACE DIRECTOR/CHOREOGRAPHER and any other credit here)

Orchestration 25%
Doug Walter

Piano – Vocal Selections – published by C F Peters (#68126)
Available at www.samuelfrench.com

Love Songs Website – www.lovesongs-amusical.com

LOVE SONGS – A MUSICAL had a workshop performance at the Madrid Theatre in Canoga Park, California on December 15, 2005.

The Cast:

Roy . . . . Christopher Holder

Rose. . . . . Victoria Strong

Ben . . . . Tom Schmid

Sarah. . . . . .Fleur Phillips

Jeremy. . . . . .Bryce Ryness

Gaby . . . . .Brianne Martin

Music Director and Piano – Doug Walter

Bass – Jeffrey Levine

Percussion – Terry Schonig

Special Thanks to our "Angels":
Jeffrey Bennett, Amanda Cagan, Emily Cagan, Tod Cagan and family, Fran Engel, Anita Guss, Marty Guss, Andy Guss, Ben Levine, Eric Lundt, Ruth Manchester, Sherry Schnall, Jane Schnall, and Peter Schnall.

A very special thank you to – Gene Caprioglio and Hector Colon of CF Peters Corporation.

Without Doug Walter's dedicated, passionate collaboration, year by year and measure by measure, this piece would have never been realized.

My love songs are dedicated, always and ever, to Claudia.

- S.C.

CAST OF CHARACTERS*

GABY BENNETT – The bride. A college senior - voice major (early 20's)

JEREMY DAWSON – The groom. A sales rep for Roy's agency (early 20's)

SARAH BENNETT – Gaby's sister, & maid-of-honor (early 30's)

BEN JACOBSON – Sarah's longtime fiance. A college poetry professor (early 30's)

ROSE CARLIN – Roy's longtime paramour (early 40's)

ROY HARNELL – Jeremy's boss, & best man. An ad agency mogul (early 40's)

Here, & Now-
A Resort Hotel in Late July

Act One – Saturday

Jeremy is stuck out of town on a business trip for Roy's ad agency, trying frantically to get back in time for his nuptials. Gaby is anxious for him to return. Sarah, who has been engaged to Ben for 6 years now is weary of his failure to commit to her. Ben has been idealizing a kind of love that does not really exist. Roy and Rose, lovers for many years just enjoy themselves (and others!). By the end of the act, Jeremy is still M.I.A., Gaby's frantic and the other two couples have switched partners.

Act Two – Sunday

As Jeremy's best man, Ben has been feverishly writing the vows for the young couple to exchange at the ceremony. In completing the task, he has a catharsis and is able to commit to Sarah, finally saying to her what had been previously impossible: "I love you".

Roy and Rose unite. As grizzled veterans of the game of love they play so well, they realize that ultimately they belong together. Jeremy makes it back in the nick of time. He and Gaby are wed.

Happy ending…

*Special note – Use of an ensemble chorus is permitted with permission from publisher.

SYNOPSIS OF SONGS

ACT I - SATURDAY

1. Overture - Orchestra

2. Lo & Behold - Ensemble

3. I Am In Love With You - Jeremy

- segue -

4. Miracle - Gaby

5. Romance - Ben

6. Love Me - Sarah

7. Hot Gavotte - Rose

8. Every Now & Then - Roy

9. The Gospel Truth - Ensemble

10. I'm Rose - Rose

- segue -

11. Alone - Sarah, Ben

12. Hurry Home - Gaby

13. Lament - Jeremy

14. Two of a Kind - Roy

15. A Perfect World - Sarah, Roy

16. State of the Union - Ensemble

ACT II - SUNDAY

1. Entr'acte - Orchestra

2. Lo & Behold - Reprise - Ensemble

3. I Don't Know - Rose, Ben

4. I'm Old - Rose

5. Carpe Diem - Roy

6. Without You - Sarah

7. Sweet Tomorrow - Gaby

8. Silly Me - Jeremy

9. So It Seemed - Rose

10. State of the Union - Reprise - Ensemble

- segue -

11. When It's Over - Jeremy, Ensemble

12. Pitter-Patter - Ben

13. Listening - Sarah

14. Say Goodbye - Sarah

- segue -

15. Only You - Ben

- segue -

15a. Carpe Diem - Reprise - Sarah

16. Always and Ever - Jeremy, Gaby, Ensemble

17. State of the Union - Reprise (Bows) - Ensemble

AUTHOR'S NOTE

This acting edition of the piece does not include property, costume, and set plots. This is intentional.

The piece has been designed so it can be performed in its most basic version by six acting-singers and a pianist, requiring nothing more than creative lighting and appropriate clothing for the characters. It can be intimate and immediate, placed in the here-and-now without traditional scenic elements.

At the other end of the spectrum, given a hefty budget and large facility, it can also be performed with an additional chorus, ("extras" at the hotel), and a full orchestra. The sets may be as elaborate as one might expect to see at a luxury resort.

I prefer to not constrain the director's prerogatives in his/her envisioning a mounting of the piece.

–Steven Cagan

Time: Here & now.
Place: A hotel.
Event: A wedding.

ACT I – SATURDAY

1 – Overture

2 – Lo and Behold

(ENSEMBLE in limbo)

GABY. I'm gonna be a bride
Butterflies aside
Gonna trip my way down that aisle
And wear this smile.

(Flashes 'tooth-grin')

I'm gonna wear this dress

(Holds up gown)

Overlook the stress
Never mind my bowels are a mess
And show some style!

JEREMY. Style and panache, a deal in the making
Kudos and cash, rewards for the taking
I'm gonna make it real
Gonna close this deal
Gonna seize this moment ahead
Then I'll be wed!

ALL. Lo and behold.

ROSE. I've seen all there is to see
Clearly as can be

I've been over-looked for a lifetime
I've seen through a jaundiced eye
Every wretched lie
We exchange at husband-and-wife time –
"Never before, nor ever again, could be such a love as ours."
What a crock!
So I've been told.

ALL. Lo and behold.

ROY. Am I not a clever guy?
If a bit too shy
To admit to pulling the strings
So many things to control
And so much to see to
Projects and schemes
And deals to agree to
I'm gonna seize the day
Have the final say
Gonna master all I survey
Go for the gold.

ALL. Lo and behold.

BEN. My muse has a tender ear
Every sound I hear
Filtered through poetic allusion (**SARAH** *gags at this*)
Abstruse? *(Nods to* **SARAH***)* Well, perhaps to her
Yet I doth demur

I'm in love with lingual profusion
All of the words I carefully choose
Intend to bestow a beautiful plan
That's who I am.

SARAH*: (Nods to* **BEN***, sarcastically)*
Lo and behold.

ALL. To life, to love, to family
To hope, to joy, to peace
To 'wedded bliss' as metaphor

Let there be harmony evermore.

SARAH. Oh, what a masquerade
   What a grim charade
   To pretend to thrill while I burn
   We've skipped my turn yet again
   I'm stuck here in limbo
   Biding my time
   Like some kind of bimbo.

ALL. Time to begin anew
   Celebrate these two
   As they sweetly mumble, "I do,"
   Without a clue.
   Lo and behold!

3. I Am In Love With You

(**GABY** *in her room –* **JEREMY** *in limbo on the phone*)

JEREMY. So far from home again
   So all alone again
   And loving you is on my mind
   I would pay any price
   Make any sacrifice
   To be with you again tonight
   (Soft) I would whisper in your ear
   While I hold you very near
   (Loud) I am in love with you!
   I am in love –

   Every fantasy is you
   Every dream that might come true
   You are the song I sing
   You are my everything
   I am in love with you.
   Somehow I've lost my way
   Among the bills to pay

And every day is like the rest
This road ahead of me
Will someday set me free
Free to be with you at last
(Soft) I will whisper in your ear
While I hold you very near
(Loud) I am in love with you
I am in love
Every fantasy is you
Every dream that might come true
You are the song I sing
You are my everything
I am in love with you
I am in love with you
I am in love with you.......

(Segue)

4. Miracle

GABY. How is it possible? How can it be?
Jeremy, so much happiness for me
Why did this miracle choose me to bless
Jeremy, do the chosen dare to guess?
No, I'm not a true believer
But I don't pretend to be
And I'm not a lover either
But, miracle,
Love believes in me
This must be paradise
Sweet dream come true
Jeremy, every fantasy is you
Miracle
Miracle
Miracle...........

JEREMY. I am in love with you.

5. Romance

*(**SARAH** & **BEN** 's room)*

BEN. *(Aside)* Affianced for seven years
To the sister of the bride
The <u>older</u> sister of the bride
Oh my –
So terse the verse,
From bad to worse
But, poetry aside –
I love you, but I'll never tell you so
I need you, but I'll never let you know
Not a word will be heard of romance
Melody nor rhyme
Now is not the time
For *LOVE SONGS*, simply lost without a voice
For passion, at a cost without a choice
What a shame
What became of romance?
Lost so long ago
How am I to ever let you know?
All of the rhymes have become cliche
None of the notes rings true
Chasin' a dream is way passé
Too bad for me
How sad for you –
Remember when the words were oh so clear?
And music fell gently on the ear?
Sung along in a song of romance
Whither did it go?
How am I to let you know?

6. Love Me

SARAH. *(Spoken:)* *"Whither did it go?" "<u>Whither</u>?" Oh, Ben…*
Puh-leeez……
(Sings:) Just make believe
Just pretend we're in love again
Let us spend an eternity tonight
Let's try again
Even though we've been here before
Never mind, here's an open door
Come in, come in…and
Love me, if only for tonight
Take me, I won't put up a fight
Use me, I'm giving you the right
But love me, honestly love me
Tonight.
Free as a bird?
In a word, I don't wanna be
All I feel is the need in me for you
So try, try again
I implore and empower you
Though my need may devour you
Come in, come in,…and
Love me as if we've just begun
Touch me before I come undone
Hold me before I turn and run
But love me, honestly love me –
No claim to what isn't mine
Blame? I don't see the crime
Shame? I don't have the time
Love me if only for tonight

Take me, I'm yours without a fight Use me, I've given
you the right
But love me, honestly love me…

(Interlude)

Love me as if we've just begun
Touch me before I come undone
Hold me before I turn and run
But love me,
Honestly love me tonight.

7. *Hot Gavotte*

*(**ROSE & ROY***'s room)*

ROSE. You are such a brute, resolute, irrepressible and cute
Such a stud that my blood starts to boil
My every muscle aches, I've got the shakes, beyond
restraint
My fevered brow's on fire, my palms perspire
I may just faint –
What's a girl to do
Seeing you as her macho dream come true?
Rub her yes, spread her thighs and succumb?
So much virility, humility, such suavity
So much ferocity, velocity
I'm overcome –
Such a manly hunk!
I'm reduced to feeble shivers and quivers
Junk!
Just a worthless pile of rubble
In trouble –
What could you see in an innocent like me?
Could it be that you want what I've got?

Are you just teasing me and pleasing me with flattery
Or does my lusty greed arouse a need
And turn you on?
I can see you're hot
I like that a lot
You're so very hot
Though you're piping hot
No, I think...

Let's not.

8. *Every Now and Then*

ROY. *(Spoken:)* Rose, after all these many, many years, can we ever stop playing games?

ROSE. *(Spoken:)* Never, Roy. It's what we do best. By now, it's who we are.

ROY. *(Sings:)* Every now and then you love me
Every now and then you break my heart
Tear it apart and make it whole again
Every now and then
Every time I dream you're in it
Any time I sing, the song is you
And every note and every word rings true
Every now and then–
I don't pretend that it makes any sense
Few are the things that do
Pleading insane is my only defense
I swear it's true
And you, you and you alone could save me
Make believe you care, invent, pretend

As if your loving me could never end
Every now and then.

Day after day ever lost and confused
Struggling to find my way
Night after night ever shattered and bruised
I plead, I pray…that
You, you and your embrace will save me
Basking in your grace will set me free
And your adoring me will never end
Every now and then.

9. *The Gospel Truth*

(The wedding reception room sung to **GABY**.*)*

BEN. Search high and low but you're never gonna find
What you think is peace of mind
'Cause you're leaving that behind –

ROY. What you call 'love' is just confusion run amok
You take a chance and try your luck
When all at once you're stuck
That's the gospel truth

BEN/ROY. It's the gospel truth.

SARAH. Keep keepin' on, don't give up and give in
Though you're never gonna win
'Cause you're leading with your chin –

ROSE. What you call 'hope'
Is just another word for 'dumb'
You bet the ranch on what's to come
And all you feel is numb
That's the gospel truth

SARAH/ROSE. It's the gospel truth.

ROY. Don't be a dope

BEN. Don't pretend there's any hope

ROSE. Don't pretend to know the score

SARAH. Don't you know there's nothing more then 'grin
and bear it' –

ALL 4: Time!
That's the only thing that's real
Doesn't matter how you feel
Play the hand and pass the deal –

ROY/BEN. Don't hold your breath
'Til it all comes crystal clear

SARAH/ROSE. For all the answers to appear

ALL 4. There's simply no such thing
As 'the gospel truth!'

10. I'm Rose

ROSE. *(To* BEN*)* What do you see looking at me
    Clearly it ought to be a soul-mate, a friend
    Someone who cares
    Someone who shares dreams
    By any other name, I'm Rose

    And you must be Ben
    Gentlest of men
    Poet and raconteur, a soul-mate, a friend
    Someone who yearns, simmers and burns
    Someone I could turn to, I suppose –
    You are not alone
    Though you find it hard to believe, it's true
    Another kindred soul, searching for the perfect *romance*

    Me too –
    We do what we must, posture and pose
    Call me if you should feel the need to –
    I'm Rose.

11. Alone

SARAH. What a night
    What a sweetly touching sight
    Hand in hand, the vows, the joy –
BEN. *(Aside:)* What a plight
    In the most poetic sense
    Rich with irony
    (To SARAH*:)* You see…
    For all the love we waste
    A profusion of despair will attain
SARAH. There you go again, oh Ben
    Don't you get it, it's your fear in the main
    Causing the pain
    Set it down, turn around and let it go
    Am I getting through to you?

ROY. Fear and pain with me always
   In my heart and my head

SARAH. What a waste of precious time
   Clearly you've not heard a word that I've said –

BEN. *(Aside:)* This wedding, this start in life
   So beautiful, 'Til death do part –
   Creation, the Art in life
   You are the wife of my heart –

SARAH.	**BEN.**
(Aside:) We are doomed	"I'm Rose," said she
We are lost, and left for ruin	To me
Where am I to go?	What a night, what a night –
Alone…..alone…….	Miracle, just to know I'm not…

BOTH. Alone.

12. Hurry Home

GABY. *(On the phone with* **JEREMY***)*
   Dearly beloved, I miss you so
   I need you here more than you know
   Traveling is something you have to do
   Soon as you're through, hurry home
   Patience is something I've yet to learn
   How to get by, how not to cry
   Hopeful and prayerful, to just survive
   'Til you arrive
   Hurry home –
   I can hardly wait to hear about your adventures
   To luxuriate in tales of places unknown
   And then, at last, to tell you what you've been missing
   Waiting here, here at home –
   Rainbows and roses, champagne on ice
   Joy in its prime biding its time
   Romance and passion, and dreams come true

Desperate for you to come home –
Hurry home, hurry home
Hurry home. Hurry home.
(SPOKEN:)
Hurry home, my darling. We're pregnant!

13. Lament

JEREMY. (To himself) My dream isn't coming true
What am I to do?

Muddle through, or don't even bother?
I'm neither a noble knight nor a guiding light
Never mind a groom and a father –
Still just a kid myself
Just a frightened boy
All at once 'the man of the house'
Suddenly old.
Lo and behold.

14. Two of a Kind

ROY. (To SARAH) That boy's a fool, that kid's a dud
You need a man, a hero, a stud
A macho kinda beast to tear you limb from limb
To shake you, take you
You <u>know</u> it isn't him –
Why don't you leave, just up and go?
Don't be naive, you're stuck on 'death row'
In need of a reprieve, you prisoner of hope
Replace it, face it
Your poet is a dope –
A sentimental little waif, a fawning gazelle
Timid little lamb, demure Tinkerbell
Tell him to buzz off
Or go to hell

Get it off your chest
You deserve the best –
And that is me, top dog in town

King of the hill
The jewel in the crown
Who sees and knows it all
(Though modest and shy)
I'll save you, crave you
'Cause I'm that kind of guy
There is no reason to resist, I'm just what you need
Master of the game, and born to succeed
Take me as a gift, and let's proceed
Grab it when you can
Carpe your *dee-AM* –
We are a pair, two of a kind
Let's you and I leave all the kids and fools behind –
We are two of a kind.

15. A Perfect World

SARAH. In a perfect world I'd seize the moment come what
    may
Though there'd be hell to pay
In a perfect world, I'd think it through before I do
What I do every day

ROY. Screw the concept of morality
    It's not for me, I'd rather take…

SARAH. Take the time to justify
    The reasons why I want

BOTH. A perfect world symbolically
    Where I can just be free to just be me

SARAH. In a perfect world I wouldn't question what is
    right…

ROY.	**SARAH.**
For one night	…….
For a song.	Or wrong.

ROY. And in a perfect world
The things I get are what I want
And what I want is what I need
Nothing special, just a swig
Of aphrodisia, sweetened with a hint of mead
Pure, unadulterated ecstasy
Nothing less will do
Not with you within this fantasy

SARAH. But in a perfect world I'd think it through
Cerebrally and totally within control
Rational and cognitive
No longer just act an a supporting role

BOTH. Selfishly free to love with all my heart
And soul.

SARAH. Lo, in a perfect world recriminations don't apply

ROY. Don't ask 'how,' don't ask 'why'
Disregard the price, it's all on sale
It's time to buy –
Why not give it a try?
       * *

In a perfect world I'd have it all
I'd own the store

SARAH. Filled with bargains

BOTH. Galore –
In a more perfect world.

16. State of the Union

ROY. *(Spoken:) A toast!!*
(Sings:) To the blushing bride, to the dashing groom!
To the state of this union-to-be
To a new portfolio! To a future IPO!
Healthy, robust and tax free.

SARAH. To eternity! To maternity!
To the state of this union-to-be

Here's to commitment, duration and such
Would that I ever could feel half as much –
BEN. Here's to a permanence, blissful security
Here's to the surety
'I'm okay.' 'You're okay.'
ROY. To prosperity! Perpetuity!
To annuities piled to the sky!
SARAH. Faith enough to build upon
Strength enough to carry on
Why then, oh why then can't I?
ROSE. To propriety with civility
To how perfect a union can be
BEN. Here's to a passion both feral and true!
ROY. Here's to a reason for hoisting a few!
ROSE. Here's to the masculine!
ROY. Here's to the feminine!
BEN. Here's to whatever inspires!
ALL 4. To life! To love! To family!
To hope, to joy, to peace
To 'wedded-bliss' as metaphor
Let there be harmony
Evermore –
GABY. I'm in love with him, so in love with him
Did you hear what I said? I'm in love!

Butterflies are on the wing
Whippoorwills whip-whippooring
Stars twinkle-twinkling above
This is paradise, this will quite suffice
What a loverly state to be in –
Sing little starlings, I hear you tra-la
Dance with me darlings, tra-lili tra-la
When he is next to me, sharing the ecstacy
All we will need will be us alone
Nothing more –

JEREMY. *(In limbo)* To life? To love? To…family?
     To hope, to joy, to peace?
     To wedded-bliss……?
     (Shouts) No!
ENSEMBLE. To wedded bliss as metaphor let there be harmony evermore.

End of Act I

ACT II – SUNDAY

1 – Entr'acte

2 – Lo and Behold (Reprise)

(**ENSEMBLE** *in limbo*)

ROY. Oh, what a man am I
  What a studly guy
  An *Adonis* poised for the kill
  Yet modest still.

BEN. Ah, what a fragrant bloom
  What a sweet perfume
  What a lustrous come-hither pose
  Oh, wondrous Rose.

ROSE. Roses are red, and roses are thorny
  Chivalry's dead
  And poets are horny.

SARAH. Oh, what a sordid mess
  Send an S.O.S.
  There's a madman loose yet again
  Who says he's Ben!

ALL. No, not again!

GABY. My groom should be on his way
  Let us hope and pray
  Such a boy, so timid and cautious –
  My dream isn't coming true
  This will never do
  Here I am both frantic and nauseous –
  What of the child so tender and mild
  With Mom terror-struck and Dad run amok
  Needing a hold

ALL. Lo and behold.

JEREMY. My life has become surreal
First you close the deal
Then it's off to heaven knows where
Completely out of your skull
With *'what do I do now'*?
Damned if you do
And damned if you don't, now.

WOMEN. Time for the simple truth

MEN. For a dry vermouth

ALL. For a shot at getting it right
On such a night.
Lo and behold!

3. I Don't Know

(BEN's room)

ROSE. *(To BEN)* Swiftly the pulse starts racing
Hotly the juices flow
Clearly, your interest's growing
Let it grow

BEN. I don't know –
Clearly you've had your students
Teaching them all you know
What of a course in scruples?

ROSE. I don't know –
All we have are instincts
Body parts and drives

BEN. How about the brain
And its drive to be wise?

ROSE. Maybe –
Maybe if one's a hermit

BEN. What if a pious soul?

ROSE. What if a fool, or eunuch?

BEN. Or a poet?

ROSE. I just don't know –

(They tango)

ROSE. Poetry is easy
   Honesty is hard

BEN. Revelry can tear you apart
   Break the heart

ROSE. Maybe –
   What if we're only human?

BEN. Surely that can't be so

ROSE. What if the world were ending?
   Would you want me?

BEN. I just don't know.

4. *I'm Old*

ROSE. Here is my heart, and my liver too
   Here is the spleen I adore
   They're yours, and what's more
   Take the kidneys I know so well
   Here are the thighs I abhor
   Take all of me –
   Every single part still functions smoothly
   Some of them, in fact, are hardly used, if used at all
   All of me is swell, although the truth be
   I'm old, *so I'm told.*
   'Kiss my ass,' I reply to the bird of youth
   Pass me the sweets and get lost
   I've room for dessert, and I'll eat 'til I've had my fill

   Hurt some else and buzz off
   Leave all of me –
   Here's my dear medulla oblongata
   Take my winsome pancreas
   I give them all to you –
   Hear my simple senile serenata

I'm old, *so I'm told* –
What the hell!
I'll be damned if I care what the neighbors are saying
(Sotto voce) Tell me again just how old you really are
(Loudly) Well, since I'm damned, what the hell
I'll go for the gusto
Do what I must though so bizarre –
These are my breasts
You can coax them to heave and sigh
They know the drill, as do I
My sweet bird of truth, all we have are the parts we own
Use 'em or lose 'em and do use all of me –
Beauty's in the eye of the beholder
Look at me and surely see the beauty I've become
Much like vintage wine I'm better older
I'm old, soooo old
So I'm told, so I'm told –
Screw 'em all!

5. Carpe Diem

(ROY's room, to SARAH.)

ROY. Not "tomorrow," sweet romancer
    Not "forever," that's no answer
    Not a "somewhere," nor a vague "somehow"
    Our place is here, our time is now –
    Taste the moment in its season
    Stop demanding rhyme and reason
    We may never pass this way again
    You wonder why, you ponder when–
    All the questions need answers
    But every answer spins its own illusion
    And then confusion –
    All the meanings and insights

Become a rationale for self-delusion
In seclusion –
Let it happen, take the passion
Let me love you in my fashion
Carpe diem
Seize the moment
Right now.

6. *Without You*

SARAH. I've got a bit of news for you
I've had it with amusing you
The time has come for me to just be rid of you
I'm tired of the hypocracy
So spare me the philosophy
I'm weary of the snotty little kid in you –
You talk too much
You sulk, you're such a crashing bore
You drink too much
You yawn, you belch
You scratch, you snore –
So what the hell am I doing here?
It's time to disappear
But, before I go –

You truly are a loser, the worst I've ever known
You're heading for disaster but you'll go there alone –
You're a mediocre lover, your drive does not exist
Your burn-off is a turn-off
I'm exhausted and I'm pissed –
I'll find another paramour
Of that you can be very sure
A macho stud who just can't get enough of me –
Ha ha ha ha ha ha………………….
I'll be the diva I ought to be
The one I'm thought to be

The brightest star –
I truly am a winner, the best you'll never know
I'm heading for Nirvana, but I'll get there alone
So farewell, arrivederci, good riddance, fond adieu
My mission nears fruition
And I'm off to see it through –
Without you, without you,
Without you!

7. *Sweet Tomorrow*

(GABY's room)

GABY. *(To her belly)* Can you hear me? This is your mommy
My name is Gabrielle
How do you do?
Precious angel nestled inside me
Here is a lullaby
Just for you –
Dream a sweet tomorrow, see it in your sleep
Plant a sweet tomorrow, sow and you shall reap –
Awake to a new forever, a place never seen before

A world only known to dreamers
A time worth the dreaming for…
More love to all the children
Hope for those who care
Peace to all who seek it
Joy for all to share –
A place filled with love, a world filled with song
A time when your dream comes true –
Everybody dreams your dream with you.

8. *Silly Me*

(Limbo)

JEREMY. There was a garden not so long ago
There did the flower of inspiration grow
Where did my moment in the garden go?
I took a sip but let it slip away –
Too much ambition leads a man astray
Too steep a price for any man to pay –
To leave my Gaby for a single day
I had her there but let her slip away –
Silly me, what a goose
I've run aground, that's nothing so profound
So why the many tears, the cloud of sadness?
Why the bogus fears?
Could this be madness?
Silly me. Silly me.
Losing my mind
Why the hell should <u>that</u> be?
I'd seem to have it all
I should be walking tall
Why not seize the here and now
Somehow, I can't recall.

9. *So It Seemed*

(The reception room)

GABY. *(Spoken:)* Rose, I think I've lost him.
ROSE. *(Sings:)* Though the light of day may blind you
Shield your eyes and let it find you
Let the price you've paid remind you
You were so in love
Or so it seemed –
As your smile belies your sorrow
What we think we own we borrow
So we dream our 'sweet tomorrow'

We were so in love
Or so it seemed –
You are not alone
And you never will be again, my friend
Another kindred soul
Searching for the means to an end
Poor friend –
You will find no end to grieving
All the means are self-deceiving
All that ends is make-believing
You were so in love
Or so it seemed
Me too, me too
Me too.

10. State of the Union ~ Reprise
(Rubato – Sadly)

ROSE. To life…

ROY. To love…

GABY. To family…

BEN. To hope…

SARAH. To joy…

JEREMY. To peace…

ALL. To 'wedded-bliss' as metaphor
    Let there be harmony…

    (Segue)

11. When It's Over
(Limbo)

JEREMY. So confused, so inside-out, so bruised
    So lost again, so weary
    So alone, so very far from home

With not a clue where home is –
When it's over again
Just the questions remain
When it's over, what then?
Move along, move along
Can we never forget?
Can we ever forgive?
How can anyone live in love?
So it goes, one reaps but what one sows
A seed, a thought, a memory
Time it seems makes mockery of dreams
Regret, remorse, remind me
When it's over again
Just the questions remain
When it's over, what then?
Move along, move along
Can we never forget?
Can we ever forgive?
How can anyone live in love?
Take heart, try and try again
Be brave though you've had a fall
Be strong, never walk alone
Love will conquer all!

ALL. When it's over again
Just the questions remain
When it's over, what then?
Move along, move along
Can we never forget?
Can we aver forgive?
How can anyone live
In love? In love?

JEREMY. In love?

12. Pitter-Patter

(**SARAH & BEN**'s *room*)

SARAH. *(Spoken:) What are you writing, Shakespeare?*

BEN. This will only take a minute and I thank you for the time
I appreciate your patience while I fumble for a rhyme
If the words can hold together the result could be sublime
I love you –
Though the patter doesn't matter we persist in the pursuit
An effluvium of chatter, very clever, very cute
What bravado! What pretension! What am I to add to boot?
I love you –
For e-ve-ry word in haste a better one goes to waste
And all of it goes to taste so why spend the effort
To display all that verbal skill, the thought of it makes me ill
And surely you've had your fill of verbiage –
(Furiously continues writing, erasing, rewriting)
Similes come and go like so many flakes of snow
So how is a man to know his 'likes-es' from his 'as-es'
No, I'm not a master sleuth, to tell you the gospel truth
I'm barely a master youth –
If I could find the "orange" rhyme
If only I were *Sondheim*
I would sweep you off your feet with every syllable in place
Every metaphor perfection, every thorn adorned with lace
But I'm only a pretender and I can't keep up the pace
Or happy face –
Pitter-patter pitter-patter
I love you.

13. Listening

SARAH. Get to the point, if you still remember what it was
Cut to the chase, if you remember how do it now
Give this a try, just speak your piece, then simply cease
You will be clearly heard, every word –
No need to rush, take your time and measure every phrase
No need to gush, you know the metaphor: 'Less is more' –
Don't share your thoughts, they're premature and so obscure
If not a bit absurd – not a word –
Deny the need to self-express
In favor of the loveliness of listening, listening
With all the talk one's forced to hear
The truth lives in the ear of one who's listening, listening –
The voices you hear should be more than just your very own
The choices are clear
It's either live and learn, or crash and burn
Don't share your views, don't take a stance
Give peace a chance
You've been too clearly heard, every word
Expand your grasp, extend your reach
Try listening, listening –
Ignore the urge to prophesy
You've said it all and frankly I'm not listening, listening –
Are you listening?
Is anyone listening to me?

BEN. *(Aside)* I love you
But I'll never tell you so.

(Segue)

SARAH. *(Aside)* Love me as if we'd just begun

14. Say Goodbye

(To BEN*)* Say goodbye, help me tear myself away
Make me go, help me fight my need to stay
Throw me out, slam the door and shut it fast
Leave no doubt, let there be an end at last –
Forget about what might have been
And never mind the pain we're in
Remember us the way we were
Remember us in love – in love…
In time we heal, we forget the moment's sorrow
Days fly by, every dawn a sweet tomorrow
Life goes on, though we hardly grasp the meaning
So will I, though this marks an end to dreaming –
Our might-have-been has come and gone
And push has come to shove
Say goodbye my love…

(Segue)

15. Only You

BEN. *LOVE SONGS* don't serve you well
You've heard them before
Neatly spun, sweetly sung for you
Only you –
But the notes don't inspire you
The words leave you cold
How am I then to sing to you?
Only you –
If the melodies and cadences are lost among the din
If sentiment is frowned upon then where do I begin?
If the M U S I C and the romance count for nothing
I am nothing –
Though I cling to my dream of you and will 'til I die

There are two things too hard to say:
'I love you,' 'Goodbye' –

(Segue)

15a. Carpe Diem – Reprise

SARAH. All the questions need answers
But every answer spins its own illusion
And then confusion
All the meanings and insights
Become a rationale for self-delusion
In seclusion –
Let it happen, take the passion
Let me love you in my fashion
Carpe Diem
Seize the moment right now.
BEN. *(Finally!)* I love you.

16. Always and Ever

(The reception room)

ROY. *(Spoken:) I adore you, Rose. No more games? Marry me?*
ROSE. *(Sweetly nods yes.)*
JEREMY. *(Enters – to* **GABY***)*
If I could find the words I'd write a poem
Rhyming what I feel inside, so satisfied
Just being here, always and ever, with you –
GABY. If I could find the notes I'd write a song
Music that would never end if you, my friend, sing
along
In perfect harmony
BOTH. I will be here, always and ever, with you –
JEREMY. Nevermore to roam
GABY. Never again to be alone
BOTH. Isn't it fine just knowing

Now, always and ever, we two are one, always and ever
In unison now and forever

GABY. I am complete

JEREMY. And I am too –

BOTH. I will be here, always and ever, with you.

ROY. Nevermore to roam

ROSE. Never again to be alone

BEN/SARAH. Isn't it fine just knowing

ALL. Now, always and ever
We two are one, always and ever
In unison, now and forever

WOMEN. I am complete

MEN. And I am too –

ALL. I will be here, always and ever, with you.

The End

(Bows)

17: STATE OF THE UNION – *Reprise*

To life – To love – To family –
To hope – To joy – To peace –
To 'wedded bliss' as metaphor
Let there be harmony
Evermore!

OTHER TITLES AVAILABLE FROM SAMUEL FRENCH

EVIL DEAD: THE MUSICAL
Book & Lyrics By George Reinblatt
Music By Frank Cipolla/Christopher Bond/Melissa Morris/
George Reinblatt

Musical Comedy / 6m, 4f / Unit set

Based on Sam Raimi's 80s cult classic films, *Evil Dead* tells the tale of 5 college kids who travel to a cabin in the woods and accidentally unleash an evil force. And although it may sound like a horror, its not! The songs are hilariously campy and the show is bursting with more farce than a Monty Python skit. *Evil Dead: The Musical* unearths the old familiar story: boy and friends take a weekend getaway at abandoned cabin, boy expects to get lucky, boy unleashes ancient evil spirit, friends turn into Candarian Demons, boy fights until dawn to survive. As musical mayhem descends upon this sleepover in the woods, "camp" takes on a whole new meaning with uproarious numbers like "All the Men in my Life Keep Getting Killed by Candarian Demons," "Look Who's Evil Now" and "Do the Necronomicon."

Outer Critics Circle nomination for
Outstanding New Off-Broadway Musical

"The next Rocky Horror Show!"
- *New York Times*

"A ridiculous amount of fun."
- *Variety*

"Wickedly campy good time."
- *Associated Press*

SAMUELFRENCH.COM

Reviews and Testimonials of
LOVE SONGS – A MUSICAL...

"I love it. It's beautiful."
- Barry Manilow

"How wonderful...it really is terrific!"
- Marvin Hamlisch

"*Love Songs (A Musical)* embraces essential contemporary relation-
ships with humor and compassion. The songs are memorable
the stories are timeless."
- Lynne Taylor-Corbett, Director/Choreographer,

"Truly, the harmonic color and lyrical poetry make
this an extraordinary achievement."
- Michael Feinstein

"*Love Songs* is cause for rejoicing! It celebrates all that is true and
lasting in life: love, in all of its optimistic and imperfect versions."
- Melissa Manchester

"*Love Songs* is filled with joyful, heartfelt, lyrical songs, characters
you'll laugh with and care about, and a story recognizable to anyone seeking love while coping with life in the 21st century."
- University of Michigan Festival of New Works Review